Henry Allen Tupper

In Loving Remembrance of Joseph Noyes Hancox,

Stonington, Connecticut

Henry Allen Tupper

In Loving Remembrance of Joseph Noyes Hancox, Stonington, Connecticut

ISBN/EAN: 9783337428426

Printed in Europe, USA, Canada, Australia, Japan

Cover: Foto ©Andreas Hilbeck / pixelio.de

More available books at **www.hansebooks.com**

IN LOVING REMEMBRANCE

OF

JOSEPH NOYES HANCOX

STONINGTON, CONNECTICUT

By

H. ALLEN TUPPER, JR., D.D.

"Not slothful in business; fervent in spirit; serving the Lord."—*Romans, xii., 11.*

Joseph Moyes Hancox.

NOVEMBER THE TWENTY-SEVENTH

EIGHTEEN HUNDRED AND TWENTY-FIVE :

NOVEMBER THE SIXTH

EIGHTEEN HUNDRED AND NINETY-SIX.

PHILLIPS BROOKS says that aspiration is a source of humility.
This is undoubtedly true, if the aspiration is after the good, the holy, the
divine.

Such aspiration, however, is not found
commonly among the most highly favored
with respect to the gifts of nature and
of Providence. Emphatically is this so,
when the prominence is in connection
with the material affairs of life. In
glancing over the business men of dis-

tinction, in any country, one is not impressed with the number who are eminent for profound piety, as the fruit of constant longing after righteousness.

There is something in contact with the material which is materializing. It does not tend to the ethical, the ethereal, the spiritual. This is the principle on which the young man was sad when the Great Teacher bade him to sell his property and follow him. But when the grace of God is thoroughly established in the heart of the eminent man of business, the very difficulty of his business, with regard to godliness, gives him special opportunity for distinguished spirituality. In his sphere of labor the temptations to violate the golden law of Christian ethics (Phil. iv., 8) are the most constant ; the sordid passion for gain for gain's sake is most likely to prevail; the aspiration to excel in wealth, in order that good may be done, is most powerful and most deceptive; there is most likelihood, as the Master taught, that the seed of the word will be choked by the cares of the world and the deceitfulness of riches. And when these great enemies of personal religion are steadfastly resisted and overcome, it indicates a graciousness of spirit, so firmly established that the sincerest humility may be expected as the crowning grace of practical Christianity, and the highest aspiration after the character of the great exemplar for regenerated human nature. This is a fulfilment of the beatitude, " Blessed are they which do hunger and thirst after righteousness;

for they shall be filled." And whom, among the sons of men, may we be more thankful for, than for the humble, pious, Christly business-man of God?

Who is a more faithful steward of the Master's goods? Who has better opportunity to extend good where it is most needed? Who is more likely to hear the plaudit: "Well done, good and faithful servant"?

These thoughts come to mind unbidden, as the writer glances at the life of the subject of these lines, who recently, in his home and native town, Stonington, Connecticut, fell on sleep in Jesus, bemoaned not only by his circle of loved ones, but by his fellow citizens, without distinction of business, politics, or religion, and by the Baptist brotherhood of the country, all realizing that the death of a good man is a public calamity, however great the blessedness of the deceased himself, suggested by the latter stanzas of the following poem, the last he ever asked a loving amanuensis to copy for him.

A QUIET TALK WITH GOD.

I sit alone in my chamber,
  And I talk with God the while,
And he seems so very near me
  I think I can see Him smile.

Alone with my dear, kind Father,
  My room grows bright and more bright,
For His glory fills all about me
  Till it glows with a halo of light.
And I remember His precious promise,
  " Come, weary one, draw near
When billows roll o'er thy troubled soul,
  And I will dispel all fear."

So I sit and talk with my Father
   In this homely little place,
And I think of the light and glory
   Of that other and better place.
When this tent I shall lay aside,
   Made clean by His boundless grace,
I shall walk the golden pavement
   And see Him face to face.

I shall see Him face to face,
   And I 'm sure I shall know Him there,
For I 've talked with Him so often
   When burdened with sorrow and care.
And my soul has gone out to meet Him,
   Struggling His word to fulfil,
So gently He 's quelled the wild tempest
   With a whispered " Peace, be still."

Mr. Hancox was converted and made a public profession of faith when seventeen years old. He was baptized by the Rev. Jabez Swan, June 26th, 1842, and became a member of the First Baptist Church of Stonington, Connecticut.

He had the gracious advantage, among many others, of the intimate friendship of one of the greatest and godliest men of this country, Dr. Richard Fuller, the great divine and incomparable pulpit orator, who consecrated his life to bringing souls to Jesus. In the spring of 1852, Mr. Hancox, who had moved to Baltimore the year before, united with the Seventh Baptist Church of that city, whose pastor was Dr. Fuller.

And it is lofty testimony to the true, noble, and Christ-loving character of Mr. Hancox that from that time until the death of Dr. Fuller he was bound to this man of God with more than triple bands of steel. The affinity between them was not only their common and constant rejoicing in the saving Jesus, but their oneness in the greatness of benevolence and benefactions. Dr. Fuller, reared in affluence and a lordly man in doing good, knew how to appreciate a spirit like Mr. Hancox', who held his possessions as a sacred trust of the Master, to be used for the Lord's children and their Master's glory. Hence his delight in fellowship with this strong business man whose will and energy no human affairs could overcome, but whose spirit, before the Lord and his brethren, was that of simple, trustful, childlike humility itself, the power of Jesus' love being the sovereign of his existence. It was not strange that the attachment between these kindred spirits should be so ardent and so promotive of the profit of the parishioner and the pleasure of the preacher.

In 1855 Mr. Hancox was called to Stonington by the death of his father. This event changed the entire course of his life, for he soon after left Baltimore, the city to which he had become so deeply attached, removing to his old home. He then established for himself an extensive wholesale and retail coal business, and also became largely interested in the whaling and sealing trade. To this he devoted all his energies until he was stricken with illness in 1895, when, without warning, God's hand was laid upon him, and his labors ceased.

But this removal to Connecticut had no effect upon the loving fellowship existing between Mr. Hancox and his beloved pastor. Letters were exchanged, and occasionally he would visit Baltimore and the church he loved so well, where his membership remained until his death. Dr.

Fuller was frequently a guest in the happy home of Mr. Hancox, whom the Doctor called his "New England parishioner." And the parishioner, keeping pace with the progress of his "Old Pastor," may be well believed to have risen, in his own experience, to the exalted plane of his human ideal.

Another testimony to the excellence of the now sainted man of God was the devotion of children to him, and his devotion to them.

Dana said he cared not if men hated him while children loved him.

Mr. Hancox gave the strength of his Christian manhood and the richness of his spiritual experience to the children, in his excellence as a Sunday-school superintendent and teacher at the same time, from

1858 to 1871. And even after an increased development of deafness, which made it difficult for him to continue to be their superintendent, the Stonington Sunday-school was unwilling to release him. Thoroughly appreciative were the little ones, to whom this man of the Lord had imparted both pleasure and profit.

During the year of his illness, "when he was so sweetly patient under the terrible restraint," children's eyes were continually upturned to his window to see if they could catch a glance and wave of the hand from the invalid who so enjoyed their sweet and winning ways. On the streets, as he was wheeled about by his attendants, they handed him flowers; and when the sleeper was taking his last sleep, the most affecting and eloquent spectacle—more affecting than flags at "half mast"; than much business of the town suspended; than a community in mourning—was the long line of children who softly marched around the open casket, to pay their last tribute of reverential love with tearful eyes and throbbing hearts to the departed one, who could say no more, as he was wont to say to his teachers: "We must bring the children to Jesus." And this loving command, how like the Master Himself, who said: "Suffer the little children to come unto Me." And still he says so, in the fact of the majority of the human family being taken to Him in childhood, which gives a perpetual freshness to the song of songs: "My beloved is gone down into his garden to gather lilies."

The doctrine of heredity teaches that human character receives its start before the individual begins his career of actual living. It is held that the complexities and inconsistencies of character may be traceable to widely differing progenitors of far distant generations.

It is not true that there is transmission of the life spiritual from progenitor to progeny. It is true, however, that many a godly parent is represented in a child who develops a character similar in spiritual symmetry and beauty to that of a godly father or mother. Does not the tender love of Paul for his son in the Lord suggest the character of Timothy's mother and grandmother, Eunice and Lois, from whom the son sprang, and by whom he was trained, from childhood, in the Holy

Scriptures? Who has ever looked upon the Madonna St. Sextus—the masterpiece of Raphael—without tracing some heavenly resemblance between the mother and child; and without feeling that the wonderful artist designed the resemblance?

But in what Christian family may not the truth be fully verified?

Thus was our departed friend blessed with godly parents, who gave him a goodly mental and moral constitution not uninfluenced by their spiritual character, and who trained him in the nurture and admonition of the Lord.

In the Stonington Baptist Church his father, for many years, was a worthy deacon, who "purchased to himself a good degree." His mother is described as a "noble, Christian woman," who gave special attention to the spiritual interests of her son, who, when she was widowed, delighted to minister to her comfort, as a dutiful and grateful son. And worthily did the son, who, at sixteen, finished his studies at New Haven, having developed "a decided taste and talent for business," and who had been associated in Baltimore with one of the wealthiest and most liberal of the business men of that city, Enoch Pratt—whom as philanthropist and man of affairs he regarded a grand ideal—become by his business tact and energy the successor of the worthy father. And not only was he thus honored in domestic life by such parentage. It is written that "whoso findeth a wife findeth a good thing and obtaineth favor of the Lord."

On December 27, 1853, he married

Emeline Pendleton, daughter of Francis Pendleton and Sarah Sophia Trumbull, the father a prominent citizen of Stonington, and the mother a woman of lovely Christian character.

The beautiful and exquisite memorials of Mrs. Hancox, who, on December 12, 1891, preceded her husband to the land of light and love, attest the reverence for her character of transparent grace, realizing, as it did, the gifts of the Spirit, "love, joy, peace, long suffering, gentleness, goodness, faith." One who often visited the home writes of Mrs. Hancox, "whose departure crushed her husband and daughter with overwhelming bereavement":

"She was a woman of lovable character; kind, hospitable, and possessed of a noble Christian spirit; devoted to her husband

and their only child, to whom she was not only mother, but companion and friend."

Mrs. Hancox was a devoted Baptist and an ardent lover of Missions. On April 18, 1853, she was baptized by the Rev. A. G. Palmer, D.D., the dearly-loved pastor who had known her from childhood and through almost her entire life. Mrs. Hancox was fully in sympathy with her husband's acts of benevolence, often uniting with him in various gifts.

In every true, earnest, and strong character there is some idea and motive of life, the one being the spring of energy, the other the point around which the character and conduct are formed or transformed. This was conspicuously verified in our departed brother.

Christ seemed to be the centre and circumference of his life. In all of his ways he committed himself to the Lord. His business life, his home life, his church life, felt the sanctifying influence of the grace of God. The unseen but all-powerful motive that prompted his daily doings manifested itself in every direction. Before he was stricken by his last illness, his pastor was left alone in Mr. Hancox' business office, and, glancing about the room, he noticed a worn Bible that had proven to be, in all of these years, a lamp unto his feet, and a light unto his path ; and pinned in the centre of his desk, where he must read it constantly during the busy hours of the day, was the following strikingly tender poem, setting forth his trust in the goodness and guidance of God :

Just to trust, and yet to ask
    Guidance still ;
Take the training or the task
    As He will ;
Just to take the loss or gain
    As He sends it ;
Just to take the joy or pain
    As He lends it.
He who formed thee for His praise,
  Will not miss His gracious aim ;
So to-day and all thy days,
    Shall be moulded for the same.

Just to leave in His dear hand
    Little things ;
All we cannot understand,
    All that stings ;
Just to let Him take the care,
    Sorely pressing,
Finding all we let Him bear,
    Changed to blessing.
This is all ! and yet the way
  Marked by Him who loved thee best,
Secret of a happy day,
    Secret of His promised rest.

Nothing was plainer than that the love of Christ was the moving power of his being. This is more than suggested by his losing no favorable opportunity of commending to others the adorable One, "whom having not seen he loved, and in whom, though he saw him not, yet believing, he rejoiced with joy unspeakable and full of glory—receiving the end of his faith, the salvation of his soul."

To the minister of the Gospel he did not hesitate to say : " Brother, do you love the Lord Jesus whom you preach ? " To the most prominent men of business, as, for example, Mr. Enoch Pratt, the founder of the Pratt Library of Baltimore, he felt it a joyous duty to present the truth as it is in Jesus. He often referred to himself as " a sinner saved by grace," the profound experience of which fixed ever before him the Lord as his loving Master, and himself as his willing and obedient servant. This was the great idea of his life. His holy ambition was to realize it; and the nearer he reached it, the profounder was his humility. The parable of the talents included an exact picture of his enthusiastically recognized relation to the Lord. He studied himself; he knew what he was and what he could do; and the work to which he was best adapted, by nature and Providence and grace, was his sacred and perpetual duty. Humbly he said: "I am a man of one talent." But that talent was a great one, as he unconsciously expounded it, when he said: "I do business for the Lord." And well could the Master entrust his goods to such a servant. His native energy and good judgment and absolute integrity of dealing the Lord blessed. And verily did he handle his property as a steward of God. It is said of him that "he was ever seeking to make the best investments for the Master."

And he recognized his obligation, as a steward, to dispense in the name of the Lord. Who in need ever applied to him in vain? What good cause, presented to him, did he ever fail to assist? Who was not made to feel, when asking and receiving his help, that he was conferring a favor on the donor? He would say when thanked: "It is not my money, it is the Lord's." And how many monuments to his princely and gracious spirit, are over our land and in foreign lands, in grateful hearts and up-built causes, in the name of

Christ ? As a single illustration : Though removed from the Seventh Baptist Church of Baltimore, more than forty years, he continued his aid to all of its interests as when he lived in that city.

The late pastor of this church can lovingly testify that, not seldom, did his encouraging words, his wise suggestions, and his munificent gifts act as a new inspiration to people and pastor. His visits to the old church were always hailed with delight ; and young and old alike sought to honor the one whose love for his church remained undiminished during all these years of absence. In the highest sense he was the pastor's friend — unselfish, sympathetic, generous, and true. He loved to invest for the Lord, where fire could not burn, water could not drown, and time could not destroy—in immortal mind and spirit. Hence his gifts to college, church, and evangelical work, as witnessed at home, and elsewhere at the north; and in the south, at Richmond College and the Southern Baptist Theological Seminary. "He loved to assist young men to prepare to go forth and preach the gospel of Jesus Christ."

But, the question of the young Nazarene, in the Temple of Jerusalem : "Wist ye not that I must be about my Father's business?" is suggestive of how this servant of the Most High did business for the Lord, in more direct service of the Lord's house. The revival of religion "which swept south-eastern Connecticut like a mighty wave," in the winter of 1895–1896, under the leadership of his very dear friends,

Rev. A. C. Barron, D.D., and Rev. H. M. Wharton, D.D., was largely due, under God, to his personal efforts and prayers, in inaugurating it. A great sentiment of his heart was that of the Psalmist : " One thing have I desired of the Lord and that will I seek after, that I may dwell in the house of the Lord all the days of my life, to behold the beauty of the Lord and to inquire in his Temple." In the atmosphere of fraternal fellowship, and spiritual longings and labors, and under the preached word in its purity and simplicity, spiritual gifts and graces were most fully developed, and questions of duty were most easily solved and most joyfully performed. In doctrine he was thoroughly orthodox, in life he " walked with God," with the highest aspirations and the lowliest humility. " He was a noble Baptist layman, who, through a long life, 'carried on business for the Lord,' and maintained the simple faith in the atoning work of Christ. . . . He was one of the most lovable of men, believed in the old gospel, and took a practical interest in extending the cause of Christ. . . . He was strong in faith and rich in good works. He believed that the work of Christ for him was so great that tireless energy in His service was little enough to offer in return. His constant longing was that he might see others entering into the grace, which had meant so much to him, through so many years. He was a man of extensive business operations; but he never lost sight of the fact that he was a steward of Him who had bought him with a price. His citizenship was in the Kingdom, and the interests of the Kingdom always found in him a helpful sympathizer. He has left with those, who knew his heart, that large conception of the Christian faith, which always comes when we have seen one in whom that faith reaches out into every avenue of life."

As the Angel of the Lord smote Peter in prison, bidding him to put on his sandals and gird himself and go forth into joyous liberty, so on November 2, 1895, and again on November 2, 1896, the Lord's messenger, in the form of paralysis, smote his faithful servant, incarcerated in the flesh, and bade him prepare himself for perfect freedom; and in the early morning of November 6, 1896, he passed beyond the portals of this world, calmly and grandly as the retiring god of day.

In a Stonington paper, dated November the 10th, appeared the following :

FUNERAL OF JOSEPH N. HANCOX.

The last sad services over the remains of the late Joseph Noyes Hancox, were held yesterday afternoon from his late residence in Stonington. The rooms were crowded with friends of the deceased, while many stood on the piazza and on the walk in front of the house. Many friends sent beautiful flowers which mutely testified to the depth of love and esteem in which the deceased was held by the senders.

At three o'clock Rev. H. Allen Tupper, Jr., D.D., late paster of the Seventh Baptist Church of Baltimore, of which Mr. Hancox had been a member nearly all of his life, led in prayer, followed by Scripture reading by Rev. Henry Clarke of Stonington. Dr. Tupper then read the Ninety-first Psalm, after which Rev. William C. Martin of Noank offered prayer. Then Dr. Tupper made a short address. His remarks were well chosen and true of the life of him who was dead. This concluded the service at the house. The remains were then taken to Evergreen Cemetery. As the casket was reverently borne to its resting-place, Scriptures were read by Dr. Tupper, Rev. Henry Clarke, Rev. William C. Martin, assisted by Rev. John Evans of Westerly. Then followed prayer, and the Committal by Dr. Tupper, a short prayer by Rev. Henry Clarke. The benediction was then pronounced.

The honorary bearers were Messrs. Billings Burtch, W. J. H. Pollard, Samuel H. Chesebro, Ephraim Williams, James H. Stivers, William P. Bindloss, John H. Bellamy, William F. Noyes.

The following tributes have been offered in memory of the dead " blessed in the Lord " :

Resolutions adopted at a special meeting of the Seventh Baptist Church, Baltimore, Md., November 8, 1896.

WE, the members of the Seventh Baptist Church of Baltimore, bow reverently before our Heavenly Father, who has removed from us by death our beloved brother, Joseph N. Hancox, on the morning of November 6, 1896.

For forty-four years, Brother Hancox was a consistent and devoted member of this church. Although for many years past his residence has been in the distant town of Stonington, Conn., yet his great love for the church induced him to continue his membership with us. Nor was his long membership one in name alone, for he ever manifested the deepest interest in all the works in which the church engaged, and was always ready, generously and heartily, to contribute of his means toward their success. No one seemed to enjoy more than he the blessed assurance, "The Lord loveth a cheerful giver."

Therefore be it *Resolved*, That in the death of Brother Joseph N. Hancox, the Seventh Baptist Church has lost a valued member, one whose long Christian life is a bright example to be cherished by us, and to stimulate our zeal to steadfastly follow our blessed Lord, even as he did to the end of his days.

Be it further *Resolved*, That these proceedings be entered on the records of the church and a copy thereof be sent to his daughter with our prayers and the assurance of our Christian sympathy with her in her great bereavement.

W. J. E. Cox, Pastor.
W. H. Perkins, For the Board of Trustees.
M. Hammond, For the Deacons.
Geo. O. Fresch, Clerk.

Resolutions unanimously adopted at an unusually full meeting of the Noank Baptist Church, Saturday Evening, November the Seventh, A.D. 1896.

Whereas, It has pleased our Heavenly Father to take unto Himself our beloved friend and brother in Christ—Joseph Hancox—therefore be it *Resolved*, That in the death of this dear brother, our community and our church lose a valued friend, with an affectionate, tender love, unbounded sympathy, and a heart yearning for the good of Zion. His life was to us a benediction.

Resolved, That we record with grief-stricken hearts his devotion to and earnestness in the Master's service, his never-failing charity, his wise counsel, his generous and unselfish devotion to the cause of Christ.

Resolved, That we extend our most sincere and heartfelt sympathy to the faithful daughter in her hour of deep anguish, to the sister now alone in the world, and to all the relatives and friends, praying that the Divine Comforter may fill them with the consolations of the Gospel.

Resolved, That a copy of these resolutions be sent to the daughter of our departed friend and also entered upon the records of the church.

Submitted by   D. W. CHESTER,
ROBERT PALMER,
A. V. MORGAN.

At their semi-annual meeting, December the fifteenth, 1896, the Trustees of Richmond College unanimously adopted, as the sentiment of the board, the paper ensuing :

The name of Joseph Noyes Hancox, who fell on sleep, November the sixth, 1896, at his residence in Stonington, Connecticut, should be embalmed in the heart of every lover of the good, the generous, the godly, who knew his private life of pious well-doing, and his liberal relations to institutions, educational and religious, in our country and in other lands. With natural gifts for commercial pursuits, improved by business experience in extensive enterprises, with high ideals of integrity, prudence, philanthropy, and piety ever before him, he consecrated his all, native and acquired, to the honor of Him, whom he enthusiastically confessed as his Lord. He was not only God's man : he was God's steward, avowedly and demonstratively. Yet, his donations to the needy, whether individual or associated, were so regardful of the gospel-precept, " let not thy left hand know what thy right hand doeth," that innumerable acts of benevolence, which characterized his life, will never be known, except to eyes divine and to hearts blessed by his quiet benefactions.

Richmond College has shared, as stated by our Secretary and Treasurer, "to the extent of several thousand dollars," in this Christly goodness of the now sainted man of God, in addition to a provision that the name dearest to him on earth shall be perpetuated in our college.   Therefore :

1. Be it *Resolved*, That in the translation of our noble friend and brother, the Trustees of Richmond College bemoan the loss to themselves and to the country of a broad-hearted patriot and philanthropist as well as one of the humblest of the children of God.

2. Be it *Resolved*, That the publication of his bequests to religious and educational institutions, in which our College shares equally with several others, gives assurance that through the future it shall be said of him : "He being dead yet speaketh."

3. Be it *Resolved*, That the example of this truly good and great man, in his conscientious and constant dispensation of the Lord's effects, committed,

by divine providence, to his keeping, is worthy of all imitation by our prospered and prospering men of business, who name the name of the Lord Jesus, and hope to hear, in the day of final account, "Well done, good and faithful servants."

4. Be it *Resolved*, That the condolence of Richmond College be, and the same is hereby presented to the daughter of the deceased, Miss Bessie Hancox, with assurances of the greatful memory with which the departed head of the house shall be ever cherished by our institution so honored by his favor.

5. Be it *Resolved*, That these Preambles and Resolutions be spread upon the Records of the College, and that a copy of them be sent to the daughter at Stonington, Conn.

The above is a true copy of the action of the Board of Trustees of Richmond College, spread upon the Records of December 15, 1896.

Charles H. Ryland,

Secretary.

For years, Mr. Hancox carried on his

person these lines, which breathe a loving aspiration, now fully met in the glorified life of our brother :

With Jesus.

With Jesus, yes, with Jesus,
Are any words so blest ?
With Jesus, everlasting joy
And everlasting rest !
With Jesus, all the empty heart
Filled with his perfect love,
With Jesus, perfect peace below
And perfect bliss above !